ARTIVERSE PUBLICATION

PRESENTS

Unveiled Realms

Compiler

Dr. V. Sivapriya

ARTIVERSEPUBLICATION

Title: **Unveiled Realms**

Compiler: **Dr. V. Sivapriya**
Language: **English**

Manuscript By: **Artiverse**
Edited By: **Artiverse**

ISBN - **978-81-997479-2-0**
Price: **299/-**

Distributed By: **Amazon, Kindle, and offline bookstores**

Published by **ARTIVERSE PUBLICATION**
Prakhar Agrawal
MIG – 83, Bandhavgarh Colony, Satna, Madhya Pradesh, Pin Code - 485005

Email id: **artiverse81@gmail.com**
Mobile no: **9179591620**

Preface

Unveiled Realms is a work of pure fiction. The names, incidents and characters portrayed in it illustrate the co-author's thought processes and personal experiences. They have shared their feelings and creativity in the form of their poetries and short stories. Any resemblance with actual persons, living or dead is pure coincidence. This Anthology is notable in every aspect of its existence for all of us.

Disclaimer

This anthology is a work of fiction. The publisher has made every effort to carefully edit and curate the contributions of the co-authors and ensure that the content is free from plagiarism. All the write-ups included in this book represent the unique creativity and perspectives of the respective authors.

The compiler and editor have made their best efforts to review, edit, and present the content in an error-free manner. However, the opinions, ideas, and expressions in each piece belong solely to the respective co-authors.

Each co-author is entirely responsible for their own work and confirms that their content is free from plagiarism, libel, breach of privacy, or misrepresentation of facts. The compiler, editor, and **Artiverse Publications** shall not be held responsible for any such issues.

In case of any dispute, including claims of plagiarism or copyright infringement, the respective co-author will be solely accountable and may be subject to legal action.

Acknowledgement

We want to express our heartfelt gratitude to all those who have contributed to the creation of "Unveiled Realms" This anthology would not have been possible without the support of our Co-authors.

We extend our deepest gratitude to the incredible co-authors who have shared their content and creative expressions.

We want to thank the entire team at Artiverse Publications for their dedication and expertise in bringing this anthology to life. Your hard work and attention to detail have resulted in a visually appealing and professionally crafted book.

To all who have contributed, supported, and believed in "Unveiled Realms", we extend our deepest thanks. Your teamwork and passion have made this anthology a meaningful and impactful collection of poetries/ stories.

About the Publication

Welcome to Artiverse Publications — a home where creativity is not measured, ranked, or raced, but respected, nurtured, and celebrated.
Artiverse is more than a publication; it is a metaverse for artists, built by art-lovers who believe that creation deserves empathy, encouragement, and a platform that truly understands its value.

At Artiverse, we do not believe in pitting artists against one another. Our purpose is to uplift, support, and honour every creator's journey. Whether you are an intern learning the craft, a writer finding their voice, an artist experimenting with styles, or a performer expressing through sound—

You are family to us.

To support diverse artistic expressions, Artiverse Publications stands on three strong creative pillars, each playing a vital role in shaping our community
Our aim is to polish writing skills, encourage growth, exchange learning, and build a genuinely accessible literary space for writers across the globe. While we often guide and teach, we believe learning is mutual—many times, we grow through our writers too.
The Word Bond directly connects with Artiverse Publications, as exceptional writers are approached to

lead projects, anthologies, and official publications.

It is an open, accessible platform where artists can share, showcase, and shine without fear of judgment. As Artiverse Publications expands, the Artisan's Asylum plays a crucial role in discovering and nurturing visual art that complements storytelling, design, and creative projects.
Further we have An Audio Club that provides a wider exposer to the storytellers, comedians and singers by organising open mics for all

At the core stands Artiverse Publications—the powerhouse that transforms art into opportunity.
It serves as a gateway for creators to publish and earn through their work, ensuring their art reaches readers beyond geographical boundaries. Selected works are officially published on platforms such as Amazon, Flipkart, and Kindle, giving artists the recognition and reach they deserve.

Now that you have a clearer picture of Artiverse as a publication-driven creative metaverse, we are grateful to have you with us. This space will grow stronger, richer, and more meaningful with your creativity, trust, and love..

This is a work of fiction. Names, characters, place, and incidents are either the product of the author's imagination or used fictitiously. Any resemblance to actual persons, living or dead, events, or locales is purely coincidental.

First Edition

Published independently by Artiverse

About the Founder

He is an emerging writer, motivated by a thoughtful desire toprovide healing and support to as many people as possible.His supreme happiness comes from seeing the smiles on thefaces of people, he touches with his words, and he's dedicatedto inspiring and motivating people in his community to achieve their dreams. He determinedly believes in the power of spreading positivity far and wide. His quotes, stories, and poems draw inspiration from both the real-life experience so for others and the limitless realms of his imagination.

IG - words.bydev

Call – 9179591620

Mail – devkumar120803@gmail.com

About the book

Unveiled Realms is a mesmerizing anthology that opens the doors to hidden worlds, untold stories, and unexplored emotions. Through a blend of imagination and reality, the book takes readers on a journey beyond the ordinary—into realms of mystery, fantasy, truth, and self-discovery.

Each piece reveals a new dimension, uncovering layers of thought and feeling that often remain unseen. Unveiled Realms celebrates the power of words to transport, transform, and awaken the mind, inviting readers to step into a universe where every page unveils something extraordinary.

Table of Contents

Compiler

Dr. V. Sivapriya

Dr V.Sivapriya M.A, MEd, M.Phil., Ph.D., Assistant Professor, Department of English, Kongunadu Arts and Science College, Coimbatore.

DEPARTURE

Parting journeys with invisible tears
Originating soulful music
Inflatable foot prints of brooding nostalgia
Besides the shadows of last glances

Packing clothes…
Not the straggling and pestering thoughts
Feel the tapping sound in the murmuring air

Desperate hope in window eyes
With distant memory rides
Leaving the scare and with care

Sometimes…
echoing with an ego….
And tremble feeling through trampled desire
Again prolonged with cherished journey…

Barren heart filled with
Loads of happiness and blast of surprises.
Numerous events
Depict the numbness of actions

Not a passer-by…
Passed the veins of emotion in our blood vessels
My virgin heart filled with untold tales

My foot steps ahead…
But my memories back!!!

Parting is not final destination
And millions of good bye…
Cherished journey with
The billions of rapturous memories.

Ms P.Mythili

Ms P. Mythili, Assistant Professor of English, Kongu Arts and Science College (Autonomous), Erode

SOUL MATE

Soul Mate
Hey, soul mate, you bring peace to my soul.
The echo of the cosmic song,
The steady voice that lives within.
You've been my anchor in my struggles.

Your touch feels ancient, soft, and true —
As if my soul remembered you.
Through joy, through grief, through calm and storm,
Your essence keeps my spirit warm.

You know my silence, read my eyes,
And lift me when my spirit sighs.
No matter where our lives may roam,
With you, my soul has found its home.

In every age, in every hue,
My soul remembers only you.
The bond that heaven's hands have made —
For when I see you, truth awakes:
Love is the soul, and the soul never breaks.

Arunkumar. E

E. Arunkumar is currently serving as an Assistant Professor at Nandha Arts and Science College (Autonomous). He is recognized for his academic excellence, strong commitment to teaching and research, and his positive approach towards professional and personal growth. Known for his dedication and innovative teaching methods, he continually strives to inspire students and contribute meaningfully to the academic community. His pursuits reflect a balance of knowledge, integrity, and a passion for learning that sets a commendable example for peers and learners alike.

THE ARCHITECT OF SELF

The Architect of Self
We are not streams cut deep by falling rain,
Nor circuits locked within a planned design;
No clockwork mechanism, smooth and plain,
But each a spark that makes the darkness shine.
The granite sleeps within the silent hill;
The wave obeys the turning of the moon;
But in this frame, a greater power is still:
The Will to bloom beyond the harvest's noon.
The thought that bends the wire, the hand that weaves
A dream from dust, a shelter from the storm—
This is the quality of the spirit cleaves:
To reshape what is given, hold and warm.
For we are not just born, we have begun,
And every breath is work that's never done.

Ms.Maheswari

Ms. P. Maheswari has over fifteen years of experience in the field of education. She is currently serving as an Assistant Professor and Head, Dept of English at Bharathidasan College of Arts and Science. Her professional journey reflects her academic excellence, dedicated growth, and commitment to her profession. Her visionary approach and student-centered outlook highlight her deep concern for the student community and their overall welfare.

FATE OF OPHELIA

Oh my sky hear my story,
I'm the lovely eldest daughter
Of the wealthy man and glory,
He filled my life with laughter.

Oh my land hear my story,
I was raised with lovely memory,
Adored by my lovely father
And protected by my brave brother.

Oh my breeze hear my story,
A secret that I wrote on my diary,
I fell in love with a man named Hamlet
He was close to my heart like a locket.

Oh my water bear my body,
My love slayed my favourite melody
My father played to make me sleep,
Now it's ended and made me weep.

Oh my fire burn my story,
Love never brought me victory,
The cut in my heart is so deep
Now it leads me to endless sleep.

Oh, my people did you hear my story?
The lovely adorable eldest daughter
Is always the first lamb to the slaughter

I'm so deep in asylum of melancholia
Did you hear my name it's Ophelia.

D.Tamilarasu

His name is Mr.D.Tamilarasu. He is an Assistant Professor of English department. He has that nearly 6 years of experience in teaching. He wants to express his opinion on society of current situation.

WE WISH A MEANINGFUL LIFE

A simple question, softly, slyly posed,
"Are you even single?"—innocent, it seems.
But underneath, a current quickly glide,
Of judgment, probing, dreams that shattering.

"Haven't assets yet!" it stings and burn,
It's our choice to make our lives,
Stop steering lives and your proceedings that
Can slowly steal away our fleeting youth.

"Even no child, better die," a cry
Of desperation, echoing in the soul.
The pressure builds, beneath a judging sky,
To fit a mold, to play a destined role.

Questions fry us without a doubt,
Each interaction, weighted and defined.
By expectations, scattered all about,
A constant measuring of heart and mind.

The single state, a target, open wide,
For scrutiny, for pity and for scorn.
As if fulfilment must forever hide,
Until a partner greets the waiting morn.

But life unfolds in patterns unforeseen,
And happiness can blossom on its own.
Why must we chase a love that's always keen,
When peace and purpose seeds are already sown?

Let us direct our life, the doubts subside,
A strength emerges, forged in solitude.
We'll tempt to quest, we'll ask to guide
We wish and a meaningful life can lead.

Muthamil Arasi. A

Muthamil Arasi is a second-year BBA student with a deep passion for literature and creative writing. She writes both Tamil and English poems and short stories that reflect emotions, values, and real-life experiences. Her works capture simplicity and depth, blending imagination with heartfelt expression. Beyond writing, she enjoys reading, music, and exploring new ideas that inspire her creativity.

MY FIRST JOURNEY....!

A journey without any expectations —
My first journey!

Knowing that the shoulders
Which once carried and raised me
Will not be there —
I take my first journey!

At the end of this path,
There will be no one to call "Father!"
Still, I walk… my first journey!

No boundless joy,
No peaceful celebration —
Only tears accompany me
On my first journey!

Along the way,
No endless calls or loving voices —
Yet I keep moving forward,
On my first journey!

From the edge of the village
To the doorstep of my home,
There is no one
To hold my hand and walk beside me —
Still, I take my first journey!

With tears
That carry twenty years of memories,
I begin my first journey!

Even knowing
There is no one left
To listen to my ramblings and sorrows,
Still… I go on my first journey!

As the eldest child
Bearing the weight of home's responsibilities —
This is my first journey!

And so it continues…
After losing my first love,
I begin my first journey
Of searching for myself!

THE PALACE OF THE POOR…!

The thatched roof of a hut
Has become the grand halls of a palace!
The flickering kerosene lamps, glowing apart—
They shine like the torches of royal guards!

On one side, the bent old bicycle
Appears like a king’s chariot—
And the broken, one-legged chair, propped up,
Serves here as a royal throne!

Here lives a king who toils tirelessly!
Here too lives a queen, overflowing with love!

Though rice and lentils may not always be present,
Never once have they sent their children hungry.

Every dawn, how many battles must they fight!
And in the end—
The victory belongs to this leader!

Yet, strangely,
The world calls him only…
A “poor man”!

GIRL…!

Unwanted, born out of rejection!
Grew up with no one to call her own,
Afraid of everything,
Doing only what she was told!

When all this defined her,
She stepped into the outer world —
Saw countless human masks!
Then came the endless chase of responsibilities!

To survive, she had to change —
To truly live, she had to change herself!
Because… she wanted to live as herself, didn't she?

And then,
When she began to love herself,
She started doing whatever her heart desired!
Turned her dreams into duties!
Embraced loneliness as her companion!

Only then did she realize —
Even the place she thought was hers,
No longer belonged to her today.

Dr. Richa Biswal

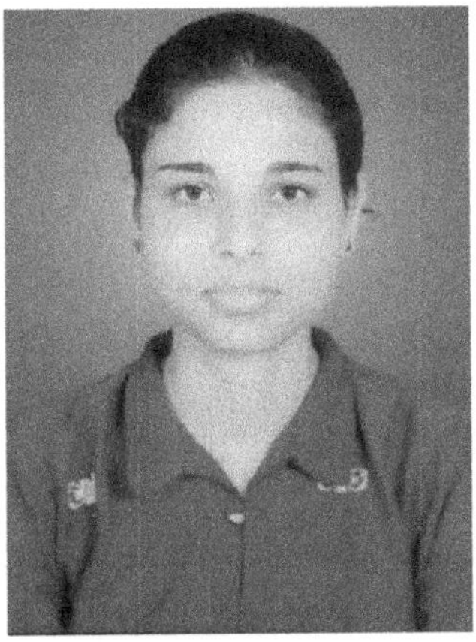

Dr. Richa Biswal is working as an Assistant Professor and Head of the P.G. Department of English at Maharaja Purna Chandra Autonomous College, Mayurbhanj, Odisha. She is a passionate academic and writer whose research interests include English literature, comparative studies, and Indian poetics. Having contributed numerous research papers, book chapters, and creative writings, Dr. Biswal believes in blending intellectual scholarship with heartfelt expression. Her works have been published and co-authored on national and international platforms. Deeply rooted in human emotions, cultural values, and motivation, her writings reflect both sensitivity and strength. She continues to inspire her students and readers alike through her words, wisdom, and vision.

SCREENS OF SILENCE

In the glow of glass, we live our days,
Scrolling through lives in endless maze.
A thousand faces, yet none we know,
Hearts connect, but warmth won't show.

Voices fade in a digital storm,
Emojis replace what once was warm.
We laugh in texts, but cry unseen,
Trapped between the "real" and the screen.

The world moves fast, the soul stands still,
Chasing success, losing will.
O modern age, your crown so bright,
Yet shadows linger beneath the light.
We are here — connected, yet alone,
Lost in a world we've made our own.

CITY OF MASKS

Beneath the neon's restless gleam,
We chase ambition, lose the dream.
Smiles are worn, like painted art,
Concealing cracks within the heart.

Truth bends for fame's applause,
Morals blur in the modern cause.
We talk of peace, yet breed divide,
Freedom's banner — hollow pride.

Still, amid the chaos, hope survives,
In quiet hearts where kindness thrives.
A single act, a gentle tone,
Can melt the world of steel and stone.

Shakthipriyanka. M

Shakthipriyanka is an Assistant Professor with a deep passion for teaching and nurturing young minds. She strives to create meaningful learning experiences for her students. She values solitude as a source of reflection and inspiration. Her commitment to excellence and her love for independent thought define her both as an educator and as an individual.

SOULS PARLANCE

Should I use a simile
Or metaphor to portray?
Couldn't decide..
I love to call this SILENCE
In my Dictionary..
Where pages are written
By Ink out of sight
Neither through any vocabulary
Nor through any sign language
Though pages are blank
And none to understand
Still Crystal clear
As there goes the reading
In between the Lines
Strong like Prince Rupert's drop
Where Achilles Heel as it's tip
Still pages are to be filled more and more
Years ahead are there to share and care
Not in a rush to finish
It shouldn't be in vain or sane
Just like toughened Invisible Thread
That none see is purely a "GEM OF BLISS"
I woke from my long slumber
And found at my tricenarian
More than eyes and a gaze
Neither recognised nor acknowledged
In silence, "SOULS DO SPEAK"
Where one feels the pain
The other to shed the tears

Yup!! In "SILENCE"
Unique things remain unnamed
Too precious are rare to be found
For it to be "NAMED"
Doesn't know, poles opposite attract
For sure those two
Do share a "Mythical Tale"
In "SILENCE"...

MAN OF POWER

For Him:
We are just frothy bubbles
He knows how to shape or size
And how much to blow
At the perfect time
Without any trace of mercy or guilt
He pops it where we fade and become none
Many more to pop and many more to blow
With a Gatling Gun
He runs the entire show
Still we hold Him tight
That's the one who is "Almighty"

Dr. Rutam Biswal

MIRRORS OF TODAY

In streets alive with neon light,
Where dreams collide with endless night,
The city hums a restless tune,
Beneath the sun, beneath the moon.

Screens that glow with fleeting fame,
Faces lost in a silent game,
Whispers echo through crowded lanes,
Hope entwined with unseen chains.

Voices rise, yet fade too fast,
Stories clinging to shadows cast,
In bustling squares, in quiet rooms,
Life unfolds, yet quietly looms.

We chase the now, we grasp, we yearn,
For fleeting joys we can't discern,
The heart debates what eyes can't see,
Bound by chains of what must be.

Yet in the chaos, a spark remains,
A fleeting joy, a love that gains,
Through fractured paths, through endless streams,
We live, we fall, we dare our dreams.

In contemporary throbs and schemes,
Lie hidden truths, forgotten dreams,
The world unveiled, both near and far,
Mirrors of today show who we are.

ECHOES OF THE NOW

In concrete jungles, lights ablaze,
We walk through nights and blur the days,
A thousand thoughts in endless streams,
Life flows in fragments, not in dreams.

Connections flicker, thin and frail,
In fleeting texts, our truths unveil,
Voices rise, then softly fade,
In crowded streets, in silent shade.

We chase the hours, the fleeting fire,
Grasping at dreams that never tire,
Through joyous days and anxious nights,
The soul still seeks its hidden lights.

The world turns on, relentless, vast,
Moments vanish, too swift, too fast,
Yet still we pause, in quiet rooms,
To find the bloom within the gloom.

Through trials, joys, and muted cries,
Through fleeting fame and whispered lies,
Unveiled realms of life appear,
Whispering truths we hold most dear.

S. Mythili

S. Mythili serves as an Assistant Professor of English at Nandha Arts and Science College (Autonomous), Erode. She is dedicated to nurturing a love for literature and language among her students. Her academic interests include contemporary literary studies and cultural discourse. She has contributed to various seminars and publications in the field of English Studies. Her commitment to teaching reflects her passion for academic excellence and student.

THE DIVINE MOTHER EARTH

The greatest gift of God above,
You fill our hearts with endless love.
A boon to humankind you give,
O Mother Earth, you help us live.

You bear our wrongs, yet never blame,
Your boundless mercy knows no shame.
Like gentle winds that cross the sea,
You guide us all with dignity.

Your smile brings hope, your grace brings peace,
Your giving heart shall never cease.
You teach us patience, calm, and care,
A holy soul beyond compare.

Planets, rivers, skies, and seas,
All bow before your harmonies.
From you we learn what love should be—
Pure, enduring, endlessly free.

Sacred Mother, strong yet mild,
Shelter every weary child.
Bless our hearts to live as you,
Kind, forgiving, pure, and true.

Anushya M

"கனவுமெய்ப்படவேண்டும்"

BLOW THE CANDLE

Smile through every compulsion around you......
Breath in the love that lies beside you......
Walk past the doubts that hinder you.....
Swing by the optimism that flies you high......
Ride along the possibilities that kccp you alive....
Slide through negativities that keep you invincible...
Fall into the mess that finds you.......
Stop by the spark that lights you.......
Dust the shine and collect your you......
Dwell into anything that pulls you through darkness
And
Blow the Candle.......
To witness the Stars around You.......

Mallika

Mrs. Mallika is a Guest lecturer in L.R.G Govt Arts college for women. She has been working from past 2 years in English department.

NATURE IS BOON AND BANE

Nature is an incomprehensible mystery,
sometimes seen as a blessing and
sometimes as a curse.
Man's life is one with nature,
So he travels his life with nature.
Nature is a wonderful thing,
It cannot be created by man but
It can only be enjoyed.
Nature is a beautiful place,
And when you look at it,
The human heart becomes very calm.
Nature provides humans with things like food
And keeps them alive,
But at times, it can also
destroy the human race with its fury.

Ms. E.UMA MAHESHWARI M.A, M. Phil

EPITOME OF LOVE

You came like a flower blooming in a dream,
You became what I was searching for
Minutes and days rendered us silent.
Memories and glances spoke with us.
Placing love in the eyes,
Within me, you...
Smiling with lips, entering with the heart.
Forever mingling with the soul,
You became my life itself.

Dr. A. Sweety Samariyal

Dr. A. Sweety Samariyal is a faculty member in the Department of English at Sri Krishna Arts and Science College, Coimbatore. She is committed to academic excellence, student development, and the study of language and literature. With a passion for teaching and research, she contributes actively to the department's academic initiatives and engages learners through her insightful and student-centered approach.

THE PULSE OF MY UNIVERSE

When life blossomed -
My shelter, my safest space
Who nourished me, gave her all, my gentle grace
To my first love, my favourite, and my warm embrace.

While a toddler -
My playmate, my companion
Who styled me, adored me, my guiding light
To my forever buddy, my charming beauty and my heart's delight.

While a teenager -
My advisor, my well-wisher
Who shaped me, corrected me, steady and strong
To my best friend, my chatter box, all day long.

As a woman now -
My only true love, who is constant, my soulmate
Who bears my pain, and my tears, my timeless pride
To my confidant, my cheerleader, forever by my side.

Through my smiles and tantrums, wins and falls - you stood by me, my guardian angel
My anchor, my hope, my comfort, my lifeline, my blessing, my heartbeat - my mother
To make you the happiest woman is my ultimate pursuit of life. Yearning for motherhood just because of you.
To my mother, who holds my world together.

Ms. S. Priya

Ms. S. Priya MA., B.Ed., M.Phil., serves as Assistant Professor, Department of English at Kongu Arts and Science College (Autonomous) with one decade of Teaching experience. Her focus is on Indian Writing in English.

LET"S SPREAD PEACE

Thousands of years have passed—
people lived, people died,
and the echoes of their footsteps
are buried in the dust of time.

Brutal killings stain the earth,
the land lies shattered,
the skies run red with silent grief.

When God created man, He smiled—
He dreamed of earth as paradise.
But man rejected Heaven's gift,
and peace was broken by his own hands.

The world weeps in quiet sorrow.
War cripples hearts and dims the soul,
it burns the land and leaves no trace
of glory, honor, or human grace.

For power, pride, and selfish will,
men fight, destroy, and fall.
Where love once lived, chaos reigns—
peace has fled, and hearts grow cold.

Who will restore what has been lost?
Who will mend what time may erase?

Before the tides of time sweep away
the final breath of human life,

let us welcome a new dawn—
a dawn of peace, a world free from violence.

Mr. Velanathan J

Mr. Velanathan J. is an author and educator deeply passionate about English language teaching, phonetics, and the art of storytelling. His writings reflect a keen sensitivity to human emotions, language, and the world of ideas. With a strong foundation in linguistics and literature, he strives to merge his love for language with creative expression. Through his poems, he invites readers to explore thought-provoking themes of self-realization, growth, and the human spirit, crafting verses that resonate with both heart and intellect.

RISE AND ROAM

Beneath the sprawling banyan's might,
Whose roots like serpents twist in night,
The tender grass, the flowers fair,
Spread out their colors in the air.
Yet under this great canopy,
No oak or cedar dares to be.

As blossoms bend to seek the sun,
But find its warmth and light undone,
By banyan's vast and looming shade,
Where no grand blooms will ever fade.
So too do men, like fragile flowers,
Rely on others for their powers,
But in that shade, their dreams confined,
Can never stretch, or seek, or find.

For in dependence lies the chain,
That stunts the soul from higher gain.
Like flowers beneath the banyan's arm,
We shrink away from nature's charm.
And only those who rise and roam,
Can find the sky, the stars, their home.

Mrs. P. Amutha

Mrs. P. Amutha Lecturer in English LRG Govt Arts College for Women Tirupur I am a lover of Nature. I am interested in writing poem. My passion is Teaching and Learning as well.

MY SAVIOUR AND PROTECTOR

Too many pains and problems,
Too much of suffering and upsets,
Too many worries and great mental agony ,
All because of too much of love and affection!
Too much of trust and belief !

I have lots of questions in my mind ,
Why all this is happening to me when God is with me?
Why all this has happened to me when I am doing good
to all ?
Why is God just watching and keeping silence till now?

Inspite of all this ,
I still believe in Him !
I respect His silence till now!!!!
I do believe that Everything happens for a reason!!!
He will do miracles I know, in a minute !
In a second !

As a human being I am tired of all these,
But I strongly believe
God is going to wipe my tears with His hands!!!
God will save me from Everything fearful !
He will purify my heart and mind by His Holiness!!!

I really wonder at myself -
How am I alive still ?
How am I strong enough to survive all this?
With all these man- made pains and wounds of love,

I still Trust in Him !
He is my only Saviour and Protector!!!

THE SECRET OF NATURE

Look at the flowers !
Variety of sizes, shapes and colours ...
Like unity in diversity!
Attracting bees and butterflies!
Blossoming like newborn kids,
Spreading their fragrances!

Look at the leaves!
Dressed in green
Dancing like dolls in the breeze!
Moving like queens
In their own world !
This melts my heart ,
And inspires me a lot!

Glance at the birds
Singing their songs with great melody !
With joy and happiness ,
Making their own tunes!
Few sing a song like these !
No composition ever
Can match a cuckoo's song !
It's just mesmerizing
And divine !

See the stars and the sky
The Moon is wandering ;
Her light shines everywhere !
Stars twinkle with brightness !

The Sky's heart is broad
Giving shelter to the clouds, moon and the stars!

Observe the sea and its waves
They are very calm
The Sun sails on the sea
Plant kingdom is there!
Fishes swim along ;
Dolphins dance along ;
Sharks, star fish and crabs enjoy endlessly !
Mermaids ready to grant the wishes!
Nature purifies our thoughts !
And brings rhythm to our hearts!
Heals our pains,
Clears our stains ,
Gives solace to our souls !
Soothes our mind
And helps us find
Who we are!!!

Nature is an emotion!
A Realm of imagination !Source of inspiration !
Object of admiration!
Nature is constant
and is the same always!
But humans????

DEAR BLACK FISH (DEDICATED TO YOU)

The moment you entered in my life
I enjoyed limitless happiness and joy
U gave me so much of joy and peace
In a very short period…… When I watched you in the pot
You were enjoying a lot
Swaying your swings along the water
Spread happiness to your fellow mates……

I was surprised to see YOU
How AFFECTIONATE YOU were towards your mates!!!!!!!
They are all alone now!!!!!!!
Searching YOU EVERYWHERE!!!!!!!
Missing YOU FOREVER!!!!!!!
They are saying that YOU are no more!!!!!
Shedding their tears!!!!!!!
Saying " REST IN PEACE, DEAR"!!!!!!!

YOU are a martyr!!!!!!!!
Sacrificing your life for unconditional love
Which YOU had and still having on me !!!!!!!!
I am a loser FOREVER!!!
Mourning for YOU FOREVER!!!

Where ? When? and How ?
Will I see YOU DEAR!!!
That is my only fear!!!

Come back MY DEAR!!!
That is my only prayer!!!!!!

HER PRECIOUS GIFT

Waiting to excite him in many ways,
She waited for many months and days,
Wanted to enjoy each and every second of the day,
With happy, joyous pleasures with love.

Hoping to do new things on that day,
Taking a few resolutions ,
Awaiting to wish him with utmost love and care,
She prayed God for the day to come soon...

The day comes,
Sweets and cakes , decors by candles,
The lights of candles brighten his face ,
Her heart rejoices and her eyes are twinkling like the stars,
Very curious to see his happiness ....

God blesses him
Showers love upon him
The crowd wish him with costly gifts
She is standing aside without any gifts ....

But there is a precious gift forever!!!
She is ready to give herself to him forever!!!
That is HER LOVE!!!!
The boy doesn't know
the value of True love!
That's how the finest day ends....

Dr V. Vani Ayyaswariya

Dr. V. Vani Ayyaswariya, an accomplished academic and literary enthusiast from Erode, Tamil Nadu serves as an Assistant Professor of English at Kongu Arts and Science College. With a profound passion for poetry, literature, and teaching, she blends scholarly insight with creative expression, inspiring her students and readers alike, a firm believer in the transformative power.

VISIONARY REALMS: THE ART OF BECOMING

People say,
My shape was simple,
A mortal outline,
Bound by fear.

But I found the fractures
Where the old light gasps,
And I walk into its singing.

Each scar becomes a gateway,
Each silence... an oracle,
Beneath my ribs,
Forgotten constellations stir,
Begin to name themselves again.

The world would bind me in its narrow myth,
Call me small, unchanging, known—
Yet the realm within
Burns like a temple rekindled.
It hums with the tongues of dawn,
With visions no disbelief can dim.

Each rising is a shedding...
Another veil dissolves into wind.
And through the mist of what I was,
I glimpse the unending story:

Not the end of me—
But the art of becoming,
Breathing my name anew,
In complete trust to unveil realms.

Read More from Artiverse Publications

In Her Depths - by Sakina Raotiwala

In Her Depths is a powerful and intimate poetry collection that takes readers on an emotional journey through the complexities of a woman's inner world. this English-language book delves into the profound themes of love, mental health, pain, trauma, and hope, offering a raw and reflective exploration of the human experience. Each poem serves as a window into the struggles that often remain hidden beneath the surface, capturing the courage required to confront one's deepest vulnerabilities. This contemporary work of women's fiction resonates with anyone who has faced emotional challenges and sought healing through self-discovery. The collection beautifully balances darkness with light, illustrating the quiet strength and resilience that emerge from life's most difficult moments. Perfect for readers who appreciate psychological depth and authentic storytelling, In Her Depths invites you to embrace vulnerability and find solace in shared experiences.

You can directly buy from the publication or can order from Kindle, Amazon, Etc.

https://www.amazon.in/dp/B0GH6MJWRH

Starting With Me

I spent so long just being small,
Shrinking to fit, afraid to fall.
But now I speak with softer grace
And choose to take up my own space.

I used to beg for love to stay,
But now I give myself that say.
No longer lost in others' view
I start with me, and build what's true.

It's not a perfect, flawless rise,
But I can see it in my eyes.
The girl I left the one I flee
Deserves my love, deserves to be.

Learning to Love Yourself Again!

Moon is beautiful, isn't it? – By Dev

It is a heartfelt poetry collection that explores the different stages and emotions of love from a man’s perspective. Comparing love to the moon—often admired for its beauty yet filled with unseen shadows—the poems reflect on the excitement of beginnings, the depth of connection, the pain of misunderstandings, and the reality of heartbreak. Through raw emotions, deep reflections, and touches of motivation, the author uncovers the reasons relationships fall apart while reminding readers that love, despite its ups and downs, still holds a unique beauty. This collection invites readers to connect with the unspoken feelings of love, loss, healing, and the quiet strength it takes to believe in love again.

Promise

Can you give me a promise?
Promise that can hold me,
Hold me till the end of my life,
Life that I want to live with you,

You and I beautifully turning,
Turning our hairs from black to white,
White like the rose in my hand,
Hand which is playing a tune,

Tune that calms the day light
Light that will make us shine,
Shine as the days passed away,
Away from each other but still,

Still remember our promise,
Promise that you gave me one day,

Day when we suddenly meet,
Meet that was maybe planned by God,

God who is keeping us apart,
Apart to reach us lessons,
Lessons that will guide us,
Us in keeping our promise,

Promise that only you can give me.

Hail Jaganath – By V Vamsi

Hail Jagannath is a spiritual love story set in the holy land of Puri. It follows two souls whose bond grows through silence, faith, and surrender rather than dramatic conflict. Rooted in devotion and destiny, this novel explores the idea that true love is not always about possession sometimes it is about acceptance.

Reviews –

Bilkul simple shabdonmeinkaheintoh, yeh ek pyaar aur vishwas ki kahanihai.

Author ne batayahai ki ye kahanidimaag se zyadadil ki awaaz se likhigayihai. Ismein Rishikeshav aur Shreejike beech ka rishtasirf do logon ka mel nahihai, balkiunka Bhagwan Jagannath par jo atootbharosahai, wahiunhemushkilwaqtmeinbhijoderakhtahai.

Sacha Intezar: Yeh dikhatahai ki kaise door rehkarbhi log sirfapnevishwaskedum par ek-dusrekepaas reh sakte hain. Bhagwan ka saath: Ismein Jagannath ji ko sirf murti nahi, balki ek dost aur raahdikhane wale keroopmeindikhayagayahai jo chup-chap unkikismatlikhrahe hain.

https://www.amazon.com/dp/B0GRBCV5WM

https://www.amazon.in/dp/B0GNKJL8KK

www.ingramcontent.com/pod-product-compliance
Ingram Content Group UK Ltd.
Pitfield, Milton Keynes, MK11 3LW, UK
UKHW021410190726
13845UKWH00028B/994

9 788199 747920